HEIDI HECKELBECK

and the Snow Day Surprise

By Wanda Coven

Illustrated by Priscilla Burris

LITTLE SIMON

New York London Toronto Sydney New Delhi

This book is a work of fiction. Any references to historical events, real people, or real places are used fictitiously. Other names, characters, places, and events are products of the author's imagination, and any resemblance to actual events or places or persons, living or dead, is entirely coincidental.

LITTLE SIMON

An imprint of Simon & Schuster Children's Publishing Division
1230 Avenue of the Americas, New York, New York 10020
First Little Simon paperback edition August 2021
Copyright © 2021 by Simon & Schuster, Inc.
Also available in a Little Simon hardcover edition.
All rights reserved, including the right of reproduction in whole or
in part in any form. LITTLE SIMON is a registered trademark of
Simon & Schuster, Inc., and associated colophon is a trademark of
Simon & Schuster, Inc. For information about special discounts
for bulk purchases, please contact Simon & Schuster Special Sales
at 1-866-506-1949 or business@simonandschuster.com.
The Simon & Schuster Speakers Bureau can bring authors to
your live event. For more information or to book an event contact
the Simon & Schuster Speakers Bureau at 1-866-248-3049 or visit
our website at www.simonspeakers.com.
Designed by Ciara Gay
Manufactured in the United States of America 0721 MTN
10 9 8 7 6 5 4 3 2 1
Library of Congress Cataloging-in-Publication Data
Names: Coven, Wanda, author. | Burris, Priscilla, illustrator.
Title: Heidi Heckelbeck and the snow day surprise / by Wanda Coven ; illustrated by
Priscilla Burris. | Description: First Little Simon paperback edition. | New York : Little
Simon, 2021. | Series: Heidi Heckelbeck ; 33 | Audience: Ages 5–9 | Summary: After a
week of nonstop rain, Heidi Heckelbeck and her friends' dreams of building snowmen and
ice-skating in the park are quickly washing away, until Heidi uses a little magic to help
Mother Nature. | Identifiers: LCCN 2021007775 (print) | LCCN 2021007776 (ebook) | ISBN
9781534485839 (paperback) | ISBN 9781534485846 (hardcover) | ISBN 9781534485853
(ebook) |Subjects: CYAC: Witches—Fiction. | Magic—Fiction. | Weather—Fiction.
Classification: LCC PZ7.C83393 Hbs 2021 (print) | LCC PZ7.C83393 (ebook) | DDC [Fic]—dc23
LC record available at https://lccn.loc.gov/2021007775
LC ebook record available at https://lccn.loc.gov/2021007776

CONTENTS

Chapter 1

THINK SNOW!

Ker-plunk!

Mom dropped a box labeled HEIDI WINTER on the kitchen counter.

Dad dropped another box beside it, labeled HENRY WINTER.

Heidi was the first one to spy the box with *her* name on it.

"What's in THERE?" she asked.

Henry looked over and spotted the box with *his* name on it. "Let me guess," he said. "Is THAT where we're going to LIVE this winter?"

Heidi rolled her eyes. "Do you really think we're going to hibernate in boxes, like bears in a cave?!"

Henry held up his hands. "Well, why not? We can each have our own PRIVATE space, finally!"

Mom laughed and opened Heidi's box. She pulled out a snowflake sweater.

"These boxes have winter clothes to keep you two bear cubs warm," she explained.

3

Dad opened Henry's box and said, "We got them out of storage because we heard it might snow today!"

Heidi and Henry looked at each other and squealed.

"Does that mean we're going to have a SNOW day?" asked Heidi.

Dad switched on the TV. "Let's listen to the weather report and find out!" he said.

Heidi and Henry sat at the kitchen table and faced the TV.

"There's Melanie Maplethorpe's MOM!" cried Heidi, pointing at the TV.

Missy Maplethorpe was the local weather reporter. Her daughter, Melanie, was Heidi's classmate and not-so-very-best friend. "Duh, everybody knows THAT," said Henry.

"Come on, you two," said Mom as she turned up the TV volume. "Let's hear what Missy has to say."

The weather reporter stood in front of the Brewster Library with a microphone in her hand. She had a blond ponytail, like her daughter, and she wore a pink winter coat with white fur trim.

"Brewster beware!" Missy began, her scarf flapping in the wind. "We could be in for the blizzard of the century! Please stay tuned for updates. We may even have some school cancellations this week."

Heidi and Henry clapped their hands and shouted, "YAAAAY!"

Mom and Dad covered their ears.

"Okay, settle down!" Mom said with a smile. "It's time to bundle up in your winter clothes. School hasn't been canceled *yet*!"

Chapter 2

JiNX!

Heidi and Henry clomped onto the bus in their winter boots.

Almost everyone had on winter clothes. There were hats with pom-poms and hats with kitty-cat ears. Kids had on puffer jackets and warm boots, too.

But there was one kid on the whole bus who wasn't dressed for a snowstorm. It was one of Heidi's best friends, Bruce Bickerson.

Bruce only had on a light rain jacket and black rubber boots.

Heidi slid into the seat next to him and whispered, "Bruce! Didn't you HEAR? A BLIZZARD is coming!"

Bruce calmly nudged his glasses up

the bridge of his nose. "Well, according to MY calculations, we're only going to get rain," he told her.

Then Bruce held up his tightly wrapped umbrella.

"Look, I know you're an amazing scientist and everything," said Heidi, "but Missy Maplethorpe said we're going to get the BLIZZARD OF THE CENTURY. And she never goofs up the weather."

Bruce shrugged and said, "I've been tracking this storm on my Super Bicker Weather Tracker. The chances of Brewster getting a blizzard are slim. But I CAN guarantee lots of rain."

Heidi sighed. "Sometimes your scientific explanations are so, SO annoying."

"Hey, science is NEVER annoying," Bruce remarked.

Heidi folded her arms. "Well, it is TODAY, because EVERYONE wants it to SNOW."

"I like snow days too!" Bruce said defensively. "But, unfortunately, we're not going to get any from this storm."

Heidi looked away and stared out the window at the dark gray clouds. Then she heard something tapping on the roof of the bus. *Tap! Tap! Tap!* She looked at the ceiling. *Tappity-tap-tap!*

Oh, merg! Heidi thought. *It's RAINING. . . . Bruce totally jinxed the blizzard!*

Chapter 3

STORMY FEELINGS

The rain drummed on the roof of the bus. By the time they rolled up to the school, the drumming had turned to pounding rain.

Heidi watched kids shuffle toward the bus door. One by one, they hopped down the stairs into the driving rain.

Bruce popped open his umbrella and stepped off the bus. He waited for Heidi.

"There's room for both of us under here!" he called.

Heidi still wasn't happy about Bruce's weather forecast.

20

"I'm good!" she said. Then she leaped off the last step and charged toward the school building. Rain slapped her cheeks and clothes. By the time she reached her classroom, she was completely soaked.

Heidi hung up her wet jacket. Even her wool sweater had gotten wet.

Yuck! I smell like a stinky old waterlogged sheep, she thought.

Then she draped her soggy mittens and hat on top of her cubby.

That's when Lucy Lancaster, Stanley Stonewrecker, and Melanie sloshed into the classroom.

"Ugh, I'm SOPPED!" cried Lucy.

Stanley squeezed water from his fleece beanie. It dripped on the floor.

"So, where's the so-called blizzard, Melanie?" Stanley complained. "Your mom PROMISED SNOW."

Melanie peeled off her soggy pink mittens. "What do you think rain turns INTO, Stanley? Give up? *SNOW!*" Melanie answered. "And when my mom says it's going to snow, then it's going to SNOW."

Melanie glared at Stanley, and Stanley glared right back at her. Then he stormed off.

"Hey, guys!" Heidi said with a wave.

Melanie whipped around quickly. "Oh, this is perfect! Are YOU going to complain about the weather TOO?"

Heidi backed away and hid behind Lucy.

Then Melanie clamped her hands on her hips and addressed all the classmates who were around her.

"Listen up!" she commanded. "I'm only going to say this ONE MORE TIME. MY MOM SAID IT'S GOING TO SNOW. SO IT WILL. END OF STORY."

Then she squeaked away in her wet boots.

"What's HER problem?" Heidi asked Lucy.

Lucy sighed. "All the kids are mad because her mom's weather report was wrong."

Heidi glanced over in Melanie's direction. She was still fending off angry, wet kids.

All of a sudden a strange feeling
swept over Heidi—something she
had barely ever felt before.

Heidi felt *sorry* for Melanie!

Chapter 4

RAIN, RAIN, GO AWAY!

It poured *all* day long.

On the bus ride home, Heidi tried to imagine if all the rain had actually been snow. It would have been up to her waist!

But it wasn't snow. It was just a *ton* of water.

At their stop, Henry leaped off the
bus into a puddle that splashed on
Heidi.

"STOP!" she cried.

But Henry didn't stop. He stomped
through every puddle on the way
home.

Heidi steered clear of her brother and the puddles.

When they clomped into the mudroom, their winter clothes were heavy with water.

"Did you two *swim* home from the bus stop?" asked Mom.

Heidi peeled off her jacket. "NO," she said, annoyed at being wet and uncomfortable *again*. "It was more like taking a freezing-cold shower with our clothes on."

Mom pulled off Henry's boots. "I'm sorry," she said. "Why don't you both put on some dry clothes, and I'll have a surprise waiting for you in the kitchen."

Henry ran straight upstairs. He loved surprises. Heidi loved surprises too, but the only surprise she really wanted was *snow*.

After they changed, Heidi and Henry returned to the kitchen.

"Okay, keep your eyes closed, and no peeking!" Mom said.

Heidi and Henry shut their eyes.

Then Mom placed something on the table.

"Now open them!" Mom cheered.

Heidi and Henry opened their eyes. They each sniffed their mugs and peeked inside.

"HOT CHOCOLATE!" Henry cried.

Mom placed another bowl on the table. "And mini marshmallows!"

"Thanks, Mom," Heidi said as she pushed her mug away. "But how can we have hot chocolate without SNOW? It's all WRONG."

Henry grabbed a fistful of mini marshmallows and sprinkled them on top of his hot chocolate. "Well, it doesn't feel wrong to ME!" he said. "And don't worry, I'll make sure yours doesn't go to waste."

But Dad was too fast for Henry.
He swooped into the kitchen and
whisked Heidi's hot chocolate away.

"One hot chocolate per person is
plenty!" Dad said with a wink.

Mom joined them too, with a cup of
tea. "Oh, cheer up, Heidi, dear. Missy

Maplethorpe is *still* calling for snow."

Heidi sat up in her chair. "You mean maybe we'll get a snow day after all?"

"Oh, Great Clouds of Huge Blizzards— please let Missy Maplethorpe be right this time!" Henry begged. Everyone laughed.

At bedtime Heidi wore her snowflake pajamas for good luck. As she crawled under the covers she imagined waking up to a winter wonderland with the world frosted in snow.

In the morning Heidi leaped out of bed, pulled back her curtains, and almost screamed.

There wasn't a single snowflake anywhere! In fact, it was still pouring rain, and the world looked like one big puddle.

"MERG IT ALL!" Heidi grumbled.

She picked out a long-sleeved shirt and jeans. She didn't bother with a sweater. As she walked downstairs Heidi heard the news blaring in the kitchen.

"Hang on to your hats, Brewster!" Missy Maplethorpe warned. "This storm is not over yet! All this water could still turn into a huge BLIZZARD. I'm asking everyone to stay prepared."

Heidi humphed as she sat at the table. "Blizzard, shmizzard."

The whole Heckelbeck family agreed. It sure didn't look like it was going to snow.

That morning every kid at Brewster Elementary had on a raincoat.

Every kid except Melanie. She wore a down jacket, snow pants, and a thick winter beanie.

"You're all going to look so SILLY when this rain turns into SNOW!" she cried from the middle of the hallway.

But nobody paid her any attention. They just squeaked by in their wet rain boots.

Heidi found Bruce and tapped him on the shoulder.

"Do you think Melanie's mom is right THIS time?" she asked.

Bruce drew in a deep breath. "No. I predict nothing but rain for the rest of the week. Sorry, Heidi—I know how badly you wanted a snow day."

Heidi twisted her mouth to one side.

"Well, I STILL want a snow day!" she said. "But I also want Melanie's mom to be right. Watching Melanie get ignored isn't at all like I thought it would be."

Bruce nodded. "Yeah, I know what you mean. It's kinda sad. Still, I just don't see any snow in our future."

Heidi sighed because between all the wrong predictions and rainstorms, Melanie was getting washed out.

Chapter 5

MiSERABLE MELANiE

"No outdoor recess today!" Mrs. Welli announced. "We are going to watch a movie about whales instead."

The entire class groaned.

Normally, a movie would be a whale of a good time, thought Heidi. *But this weather is just plain gross!*

As the day wore on, Heidi noticed something strange *besides* the never-ending rain. There was a gray cloud hanging over Melanie Maplethorpe.

It was not a real gray cloud, of course. Heidi knew that was a figure of speech. Melanie just wasn't acting like her normal bossy, annoying self. She was actually being *quiet*.

During reading time Melanie hid behind her book. During math she picked at the tape on her number line the whole  time. During the movie she doodled snowflakes on sheets of paper, then balled them up when she was done.

When the last bell rang, Melanie didn't rush to meet her friends. She stayed at her desk.

"Melanie, school's over for the day," Mrs. Welli said. "We'll see you tomorrow."

Then Melanie slowly got up and pushed in her chair. "That's what I'm afraid of," she mumbled to herself.

Heidi slung her backpack over her shoulder and headed for the bus. *I wonder what's wrong with Melanie.*

Heidi thought about it the whole ride home. In fact, she didn't even notice she was sitting next to Bruce on the bus until he tapped her on the arm.

"Hey, Heidi, I'm sorry again," he said. "I know you were hoping for a snow day, and all you got was a rainy week."

Heidi blinked and realized that if she was so upset about the rain, then imagine how Melanie must have felt when the whole school blamed her for her mom's weather forecast!

And even though Melanie and Heidi weren't exactly best friends, Heidi still didn't think Melanie deserved to be teased about some silly weather.

A plan began to hatch in Heidi's mind.

"That's it, Bruce!" she exclaimed. "You're a genius!"

Bruce looked very, very confused. "WHAT? I am? WHY?"

The school bus eased to a stop, and Heidi raced down the aisle.

"I'll fill you in later," she called over her shoulder.

Heidi didn't even notice the rain on the way home from the bus stop.

All Brewster needs is a snowstorm. Then Missy Maplethorpe's weather forecast will be right, and kids will stop bugging Melanie, she thought. *And all Melanie needs is a little magic in her life!*

Chapter 6

SNOW TIME!

Heidi zoomed in the back door and slid smack into her mom.

"Not so fast!" said Mom, blocking the entryway.

Heidi froze. *Oh no! Does she know I'm up to MAGIC?*

Mom tapped her foot on the tiles.

"Off with those muddy boots!" she said sternly. "I don't want tracks all over the house."

Heidi sighed in relief. "No problem, Mom!" she said as she yanked off her boots and hung up her jacket. "I'm heading upstairs to dry off and do some . . . um, reading."

Then Heidi charged to her room and pulled her *Book of Spells* out from under the bed.

She checked the Contents page and found a whole chapter on winter. There were spells about ice-skating, spells about snow animals, and spells about frozen clouds. She even found a spell about winter fairies.

❄ Winter Spells

❄ Ice-Skating
❄ Snow Animals
❄ Frozen Clouds
❄ Winter Fairies

Finally she came across a spell called Snow Time! She read it over.

Snow Time!

Do you wish it would snow?
Maybe you want to go
sledding. Or perhaps you'd
like to build a snowman. Or
could it be that you wish all
the rainy weather would turn
into a huge snowstorm? If
winter is letting you down,
then this is the spell for you!

Ingredients:

1 snow globe

2 tablespoons of silver glitter

5 ice cubes

gather the ingredients into a bowl. Hold your Witches of Westwick medallion in one hand, and hold your other hand over the mix. Chant the following spell:

WINTRY WINDS GUST AND BLOW!

SNOWFLAKES SPARKLE TO AND FRO!

HEAR ME CAST THIS SPELL FOR SNOW!

Heidi gathered the ingredients. She paused for a moment while holding her favorite little snow globe. It had been a gift from Aunt Trudy. With a little shake, the snowflakes swirled around the tiny gingerbread house inside.

You are going to help make real snow now, Heidi thought cheerfully.

Then she placed the snow globe in the bowl with the other ingredients.

Heidi grabbed her medallion and cast the spell.

WHOOSH! Glitter twinkled in the air and then vanished. Heidi smiled triumphantly.

"There's no time like SNOW TIME!"
she sang to herself. Then she hippity-
hopped downstairs.

In the kitchen Mom and Dad were
packing Heidi's and Henry's winter
clothes *back* into their boxes.

"I wouldn't put our winter stuff away yet!" Heidi advised.

Mom and Dad looked at Heidi.

"Why not?" Dad asked.

A frosty smile swept over Heidi's face. "Let's just say I have a funny feeling that snow is in the air."

Chapter 7

A SPELL COME TRUE

The next morning Heidi jumped out of bed and ran to the window. This time she clapped her hands. The whole yard was frosted with fluffy white snow—even the patio chairs had puffy white snow cushions. The tree house was iced with snow too.

And, best of all, it was *still* snowing like crazy.

Oh, what a spell come true! Heidi thought. Then she ran out of her room and down the hall.

"It's SNOWING!" she sang. "It's SNOWING!"

She threw open Henry's bedroom
door and continued her song, which
was more like screaming now.

"HENRY, IT'S SNOWING!" she called,
"GET UP, GET UP, GET UP!"

Henry sat
up in bed and
looked out the
window.

"YAY!" he
cried.

"It's SNOWING!" they both shouted
as they headed downstairs to the
kitchen.

Dad was making his famous winter biscuits and gravy for breakfast.

"Do we have school?" hollered Heidi.

Mom switched on the TV. Today Missy Maplethorpe was standing beside a snowbank with her microphone.

"Oh, what a beautiful morning, my dear Brewster!" she said cheerfully. "Winter has *finally* arrived—just as I promised!"

Heidi smirked, knowing it was her spell that had brought the snow. Then she waited to hear about school.

"Attention, Brewster students. I have a very important update. School has been canceled! It's a snow day!" announced the weather reporter.

Heidi and Henry hooted and danced around the kitchen table. As usual, Mom had to turn up the volume so she could hear the rest of the news.

"The hills at the park are ready for sledding!" said Missy. "The town pond is open for ice-skating! And it's a perfect day to play in a winter wonderland!"

Dad set plates on the table. Heidi and Henry finally settled down to eat.

"I want to go outside!" said Heidi.

"Me too!" agreed Henry. "May Dudley come over?"

Mom nodded. "Yes and yes, as soon as you finish breakfast and get ready."

After breakfast Heidi picked out clothes from her winter box and got dressed. The doorbell rang just as she was admiring her outfit in the mirror.

"Heidi!" called Mom from the front door. "Bryce Beltran and Melanie Maplethorpe are here! They want you to go to the park with them!"

Heidi froze.

Wait, did Mom just say Melanie Maplethorpe is HERE? she wondered. *At my house?*

Chapter 8

THE SNOWFLAKE BLUES

"Don't you LOVE snow days?" cried Bryce. "You can catch snowflakes on your tongue!" She stuck out her tongue.

Heidi did the same and caught a snowflake too. It was tiny and cold. Then she glanced at Melanie.

She wasn't even trying to catch a snowflake. She just stared at the white flakes landing on her pink mittens.

The girls made snow tracks all the way to the park.

"Melanie, your mom was really right about this snowstorm!" said Bryce. "She's the absolute BEST."

Melanie barely nodded, but Bryce didn't notice. She was too excited about the snow.

Heidi noticed, though. It was like the gray cloud from yesterday was still hanging over Melanie.

Hmm. I wonder why my snowstorm spell isn't helping, Heidi thought.

The girls walked through the gate and into the park. Lots of kids were already there.

"Let's build a snowman!" Bryce suggested. "I know the perfect spot. Follow me!"

Heidi and Melanie tramped along behind Bryce. On the way Heidi spied Lucy and Bruce. They waved to Heidi.

"I'll be right back!" Heidi said as she zipped over to see them.

"There you are!" Lucy said. "We called you this morning, but you had already left for the park with Bryce and Melanie. What's going ON? We thought your mom was pranking us!"

Heidi laughed.

"They just showed up at my house this morning," she explained. "I was pretty shocked too. And you won't believe what else! Something's WRONG with Melanie!"

Lucy and Bruce giggled.

"That's not hard to believe!" Lucy said. "I'd say there's A LOT wrong with Melanie."

But Heidi didn't laugh. She was actually kind of worried about Melanie. "Seriously, you guys, something's really off," she said. "Melanie's not acting like herself. She's not bragging OR being snooty. She's barely even talking."

"Well, that sounds like a change for the better!" Bruce noted. "But what I DON'T understand is how her mom was RIGHT about this snowstorm. I was sure it was going to rain."

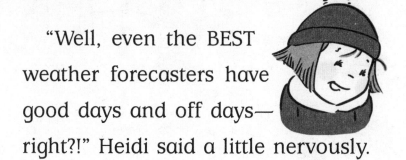

"Well, even the BEST weather forecasters have good days and off days—right?!" Heidi said a little nervously.

Lucy rolled her eyes and said, "Would you two forget about the weather forecast and just enjoy the SNOW? It's perfect for sledding and building igloos!"

Heidi bent down and picked up a clump of snow. Then she  packed it into a ball and threw it at Bruce. *Splat!* It hit him in the arm.

"It's pretty good
for SNOWBALLS, too!"
she said.

So Bruce packed his own
snowball and whipped it at Heidi.
The snowball sailed over her head.
Heidi turned around and watched it
land near Melanie. She was standing
all by herself in the snow.

Heidi turned to Lucy and Bruce. "Hey, I know this is going to sound really weird, but I've got to go!" she announced. "There's a frosty situation that needs my help!"

Then Heidi ran back to Melanie.

"I wonder what's gotten into HER?" said Lucy.

Bruce shrugged. "Who knows? Maybe Heidi has developed a soft spot for Melanie."

When Heidi reached Melanie, she saw that Bryce and Stanley were there too. They were building a snowman and had already rolled three snowballs for the body.

"Will you guys help me stack these?" asked Bryce.

Stanley leaped into action. He wrapped his arms around the middle snowball and lifted it.

"OOMPH!" Stanley plunked the snowball on top of the base.

Then Bryce scooped up the smaller snowball. She stood on tiptoes and placed the head on top of the snowman.

"Ta-da!" she cried. "Now we need ARMS!"

"Oh, there are some great sticks by those trees!" Stanley cheered.

Bryce and Stanley ran off to find sticks for the snowman's arms, leaving Heidi alone with Melanie.

"So, uh, nice snow day, huh?" Heidi asked.

"I guess," mumbled Melanie.

A few more moments of silence passed between the two girls until Heidi couldn't stand it anymore.

"Melanie," she said, "I'm the last person you would expect to ask you this, but . . . is everything okay?"

Melanie looked away and said, "What's it to you? And what makes you think I'd tell YOU anything?"

Heidi watched the snow fall between them. "You DON'T have to tell me anything if you don't want to. I'm just here to listen if you need it."

Melanie kicked the snow in front of her. "Well, how would you like it if everyone was mad at you over a DUMB weather report?"

Heidi shook her head. "I have no idea what that feels like. Is it hard?"

"Yes! It's absolutely AWFUL!" Melanie said. "And now, because it DID snow, everyone's acting like my best friend. It makes me not want to hang out with anyone."

Melanie sniffled, trying to hold back tears, and wiped her face with the back of her mitten.

Oh no! Heidi thought. *My snow spell was supposed to help Melanie feel better, not worse! Now all her friends are acting like nothing big happened . . . but they really hurt her feelings!*

Heidi had a new idea. "If you don't want to hang out with anyone, then why don't we just LEAVE?"

Melanie raised both eyebrows. "Leave? I'd love to, but we can't just ditch Bryce and Stanley— CAN we?"

Heidi smiled slyly. "I'll take care of them!"

She ran over to Bryce and Stanley and talked to them. One minute later they each gave Melanie a mitten-covered thumbs-up.

Heidi raced back and announced, "We're all set!"

Melanie wrinkled her brow. "What kind of magic did you use over there?"

"It's not magic." Heidi laughed. "I told them I forgot something at home, and you were going with me to get it."

Melanie smiled a half smile. "My mom would call that a snow job."

Heidi giggled. "Yup, and it totally worked."

SNOW ANGELS

At home Heidi's mom stirred hot chocolate for the girls. Then she set a can of whipped cream *and* a bowl of mini marshmallows on the table.

Melanie sprinkled lots of marsh-mallows on top of her hot chocolate. Then she swirled in whipped cream.

"Wanna watch a movie?" asked Heidi, squirting some whipped cream into her mouth.

Melanie nodded and laughed at Heidi. "Only if you'll share that whipped cream."

Heidi handed the can to Melanie, who squirted a huge glob into her mouth. Then the girls carried their hot chocolate to the family room and picked out a movie.

"Wait, we're missing something," Heidi said.

Then she went to the linen closet and grabbed two puffy quilts. She offered the pink one to Melanie. The girls wrapped themselves up and watched the movie.

As the credits rolled, Henry and Dudley tromped into the family room.

Henry's jaw dropped when he saw Melanie next to his sister.

"What are YOU doing here?" he asked.

Heidi shot a look at Henry.

"I mean, why aren't you guys at the park?" he corrected himself. "It's an epic snow day!"

Melanie sat up on the couch. "You know what? I think snow days are OVERRATED," she  said, kicking her legs out  from under her quilt. "Besides, we had a great time RIGHT HERE."

This time Heidi's mouth dropped open.

But Melanie didn't notice. Instead, she scooted off the couch and said,

"I should probably get going."

"That's cool. I can walk you home," Heidi suggested.

The girls got their jackets and boots from the mudroom and bundled up. Then they ran into the front yard.

"You know what makes a snow day official?" Melanie asked. "Snow angels!"

Melanie walked into the middle of the yard and lay down on her back.

Then she began to sweep her arms and legs across the snow, as if she was doing jumping jacks.

"Are you going to stand there?" Melanie asked. "Or are you going to join the fun?"

Heidi didn't need to be asked twice. She flopped beside Melanie and made her own.

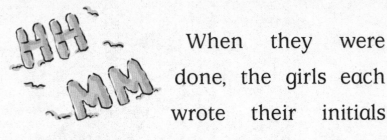

When they were done, the girls each wrote their initials beside their angels.

As they traveled down the sidewalk, Melanie said, "Thanks for today. I had a good time."

"Me too!" said Heidi. "And I'm glad you're feeling better."

Heidi knew that she might never be best friends with Melanie. But at least they could be snow angel friends today.

Then the girls walked next to each other without saying another word. Instead, they both watched the beautiful snow falling around them.

Check out the next book starring

HEIDI HECKELBECK

Tick-tock!

Tick-tock!

Tick-tock!

Heidi and her best friend, Lucy Lancaster, stared at the clock in their classroom. Their teacher, Mrs. Welli, had given the class Choice Time until the end of the day. The girls had chosen to watch the clock.

An excerpt from *Heidi Heckelbeck and the Wild Ride*

"Our THREE-DAY weekend starts in a few minutes!" said Heidi.

Lucy muffled a squeal with the palm of her hand.

Bruce Bickerson sat across from the girls. He was reading a book called *All About Snakes*. "What are you guys doing?" he asked.

"We're watching the clock until school lets out," said Heidi without looking at him.

"I can see that," said Bruce. "But why?"

This time the girls took their eyes off the clock.

An excerpt from *Heidi Heckelbeck and the Wild Ride*

"Because we're going to Wacky Wonders Adventure Park this weekend!" said Lucy.

Heidi bounced in her seat. "Yeah! It has rides, games, and an INDOOR water park!"

Lucy nodded excitedly. "Plus their Wonder Thunder roller coaster goes a hundred miles per hour AND upside down!"

Bruce's eyes widened. "COOL!" he said. "I've seen the Wacky Wonders ads on TV. Isn't it far from here?"

"Yeah," said Lucy, "but that means we're going on a ROAD TRIP!"

An excerpt from *Heidi Heckelbeck and the Wild Ride*